WITHDRAWN

To Laura Renker, Chris Haeffner, Ruth Burman, Mimi Flaherty, Melissa Lightle, and Matthew Winner and my friends at Ducketts Lane Elementary

Published by Charlesbridge
85 Main Street
Watertown, MA 02472
(617) 926-0329
www.charlesbridge.com

Library of Congress Cataloging-in-Publication Data
Biedrzycki, David, author.
    Breaking news: bears to the rescue/David Biedrzycki.
    pages cm
    Summary: In this story, told in the form of a television broadcast,
the bears and their cub catch two escaping prisoners who are hiding
at the carnival.
    ISBN 978-1-58089-624-5 (reinforced for library use)
    ISBN 978-1-60734-823-8 (ebook)
    ISBN 978-1-60734-824-5 (ebook pdf)
1. Bears—Juvenile fiction.  2. Escaped prisoners—Juvenile fiction.
3. Carnivals—Juvenile fiction.  4. Television broadcasting—Juvenile
fiction. [1. Bears—Fiction.  2. Fugitives from justice—Fiction.
3. Carnivals—Fiction.  4. Television broadcasting—Fiction.
5. Humorous stories.]  I. Title.  II. Title: Bears to the rescue.

PZ7.B4745Bt 2016
[E]—dc23     2014049635

Printed in China
(hc) 10 9 8 7 6 5 4 3 2 1

Illustrations done in Adobe Photoshop
Display type set in The Sans by Luc as de Groot
Text type set in Stripwriter by Typotheticals
Color separations by Colourscan Print Co Pte Ltd, Singapore
Printed by C&C Offset Printing Co. Ltd. in Shenzhen, Guangdong, China
Production supervision by Brian G. Walker
Designed by Diane M. Earley

BREAKING NEWS  FELINE FELON AT LARGE. CAT HAS NOT BEEN DECLAWED.

CITY POUND
SUSPECT PROFILE
001

18"

12"

6"

OPEN

Winnie's
MENU

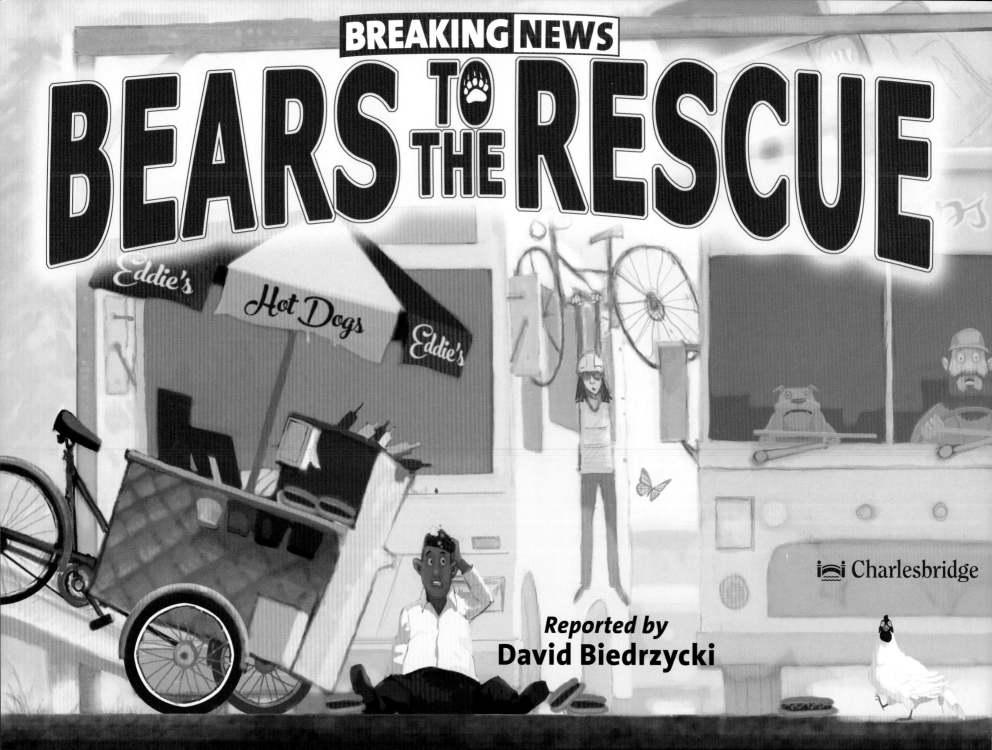

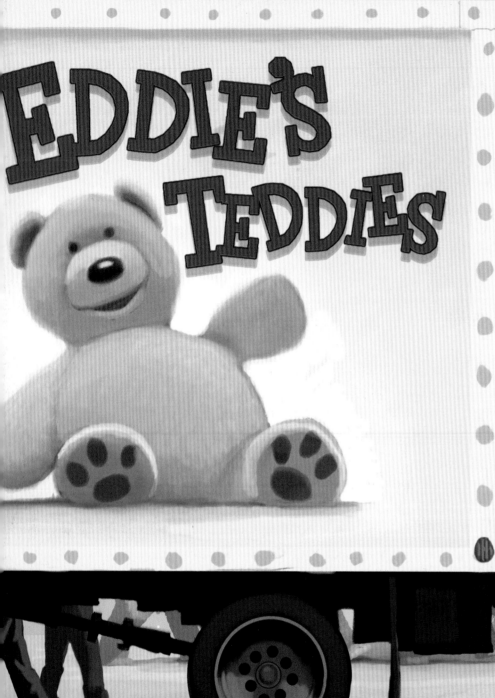

BREAKING NEWS SHORTAGE OF PRIZES AT CARNIVAL

AND RABBIT ABOUT DISAPPEARING WALLETS.

BEARS LAST SEEN ON ROLLER COASTER. EXPERTS

BEARS HAVE LEFT RIDES AND ARE TRYING

THEIR LUCK AT CARNIVAL GAMES.

3

GAME ATTENDANT REPORTS THAT BEARS

ARE PICKY ABOUT PRIZES.

CROOKS AND FOILS ROBBERY.    BREAKING NEWS

REUNITES CUB WITH PARENTS.  BREAKING NEWS

**ARE THERE ALIENS LIVING AMONG US?**